Fairies

Fairies

A CELEBRATION OF PIXIES, SPIRITS, NYMPHS AND BROWNIES

Dominic Connolly

amber
BOOKS

Published by
Amber Books Ltd
United House
London N7 9DP
United Kingdom
www.amberbooks.co.uk
Facebook: amberbooks
YouTube: amberbooksltd
Instagram: amberbooksltd
X(Twitter): @amberbooks

ISBN: 978-1-83886-456-9

Project Editor: Anna Brownbridge
Designer: Keren Harragan
Picture Research: Terry Forshaw

Printed in China

Contents

Introduction

Ever since humans began telling stories, they have been telling them about fairies. Cultures across the planet have felt the need to explain the unexplainable – and to understand the world around them – and the 'little people' have helped them do this. Although there are physical as well as behavioural differences between fairies from different parts of the world, there exist common themes among them. Many are protectors of nature, as human existence depends on bountiful environments; while others help

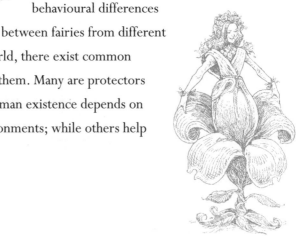

dreams and aspirations come true. There are also those who help people with their chores and work.

Then there are those associated with fertility, and those linked to death. In fact, the common popular image of fairies these days – winged, female and benevolent – belies how fairies have represented the whole range of human nature. Many fairies are mischievous, others flit between good and bad, while a few are pure evil. And they often come in the male form and have no ability to fly.

Whatever their nature, they are a colourful addition to human culture. And, from folk tales, they have woven their way into all forms of written, visual and aural art forms.

Our world would be so much lesser without fairies.

Fairies from
Literature

Shakespeare did much to popularize fairies by writing *A Midsummer Night's Dream*, which relies heavily on them. Later, other writers and artists, particularly in and after the Victorian era, latched on to the romance of some fairy stories. These arguably sanitized takes on fairies were compounded in the 20th century with the likes J.M. Barrie's Tinker Bell from *Peter Pan*, particularly in her Disney incarnation. However, more recent works, such as the Harry Potter series, have returned to more complex fairies.

Illustration of the Fern Fairy in Keepsake for the Young – A Book of Amusement *by Aunt Friendly from 1880*

It

 n E. Nesbit's 1902 novel *Five Children and It*, a group of youngsters discover a sand-fairy in a gravel pit. The sand-fairy – the 'It' of the title – is what Nesbit calls a Psammead, which is similar in name to the dryad, naiad and oread nymphs of Greek mythology, but looks grotesque not beautiful. The story was turned into a 2004 film starring Freddie Highmore, Kenneth Branagh and Tara Fitzgerald, with Eddie Izzard as the voice of 'It'.

Once upon a time…
The Psammead found in the gravel pit has the ability to grant wishes, which all go comically wrong.

Origins:
In the months before the *Five Children and It* novel was released, segments that would go on to make it up appeared in *Strand* magazine, under the title *The Psammead, or the Gifts*.

In popular culture:
There have been a number of stage and television adaptations of *Five Children and It*, including a Japanese anime version that ran for 78 episodes.

A wooden sculpture of The Psammead, a sand fairy from Five Children and It *in southeast London*

"Fairy-tales and magic, are, so say the grown-ups, not true at all. Yet they are so easy to believe, especially when you see them happening."

— E. Nesbit

"Fairies do not make a strong distinction between the animate and the inanimate. They believe that stones, doors, trees, fire, clouds and so forth all have souls and desires, and are either masculine or feminine."

— Susanna Clarke

An impression of The Gentleman with the Thistle-down Hair from Jonathan Strange & Mr Norrell

The Gentleman with Thistledown Hair

I n Susanna Clarke's 2004 novel *Jonathan Strange & Mr Norrell*, the Gentleman with the Thistledown Hair is the ruler of several fairy kingdoms. He has long, silvery hair, 'pale, perfect' skin, bright blue eyes and dark, perfectly formed eyebrows that end in an upward flourish. *Jonathan Strange & Mr Norrell* – about magic in the time of the Napoleonic Wars – was Clarke's debut novel and took 10 years to write.

Once upon a time...
Susanna Clarke's inspiration for *Jonathan Strange & Mr Norrell* came, she says, "in a kind of waking dream".

Origins:
The specific characteristics of the Gentleman with the Thistledown Hair were brought to life in the book by illustrator Portia Rosenberg.

In popular culture:
Marc Warren played the Gentleman with the Thistledown Hair in the 2015 BBC TV adaptation of *Jonathan Strange & Mr Norrell*, starring alongside Bertie Carvel, Eddie Marsan, Samuel West, Charlotte Riley and Paul Kaye.

The Iris Fairy

he iris takes its name from the Greek word for 'rainbow'. Iris is also the Greek goddess of the rainbow, so for thousands of years there has been a personification of it in human – or super-human – form. Many artists and writers have paired irises with fairies and, in the early 20th century, British illustrator and poet Cicely Mary Barker chose it as one of the plants for her Flower Fairies books, influencing many other creative people.

Once upon a time...
Cicely Mary Barker suffered from epilepsy and did not go to school, so spent much of her childhood painting and drawing.

Origins:
The Victorian artist and write Kate Greenaway – known for her illustrations in children's books – heavily influenced Cicely Mary Barker

In popular culture:
In 2014 – Transport for London's 'Year of the Bus' – a sculpture of a London double-decker was adorned with Flower Fairies artwork and stationed at the Whitgift Shopping Centre in Croydon, the area where Cicely Mary Barker was born.

*A fairy with iris flowers, painted by Czech
art nouveau artist Alfons Marie Mucha*

*"No need for journeying,
Seeking afar:
Where there are flowers,
There fairies are!"*

— *Cicely Mary Barker*

> "I was Fairy Lavender. I loved it. It was good training for theatre."

— *Actress Sarah Snook, on being a children's entertainer in her youth*

*A fairy with lavender flowers surrounded by butterflies
and on the back of a bird*

The Lavender Fairy

he popularity of lavender as a plant, with its many uses, has led it to be adopted by those who want to stylize fairies in stories and artwork. Cicely Mary Barker painted a Lavender Fairy and USA-produced dolls of lavender fairies have been made, standing more than 11 inches tall. Lavender fairies also appear on ceramic plates and there are blogs written about them.

Once upon a time…

The poem next to Cicely Mary Barker's illustration of the Lavender Fairy quotes the 17th century folk song *Lavender's Blue*, but opting for an older 'diddle, diddle' refrain rather than the more common 'dilly, dilly'.

Origins:

Lavender's Blue, which has come to be used as a nursery rhyme, started out as a bawdy song with verses celebrating sex and drinking.

In popular culture:

Cicely Mary Barker's Lavender Fairy appears on YouTube, with a picture book, *Lavender Finds a Friend*, being read out loud and the pages being turned for viewers to see.

The Orchid Fairy

ypes of orchids flower in all parts of the world, except in very icy climes, so they have been embraced by many cultures, often becoming the national flower of countries. Cicely Mary Barker chose two types of orchids to be represented in her fairy books – the straightforward 'orchis' and the 'bee orchis' – helping to popularize the association of orchids and fairies.

Once upon a time…
Cicely Mary Barker modelled the fairies
on the children that attended her sister
Dorothy's kindergarten.

Origins:
Cicely Mary Barker's Flower Fairies are pictured
in costumes based on their respective flower.
Her illustrations of plants are known for their
botanical accuracy.

In popular culture:
An orchid fairy has her own book in Rainbow
Magic's *Petal Fairies* range. Its credited author,
Daisy Meadows, was the most borrowed writer
at UK libraries in 2010.

"An orchid in a deep forest sends out its fragrance even if no one is around to appreciate it."

– Confucius

A female fairy with sets of wings sitting on a purple orchid flower in woodland

"Fairies are invisible and inaudible like angels. But their magic sparkles in nature."

— Lynn Holland

A poppy fairy, in red, and a cornflower fairy, in blue, with some woodland creatures

The Poppy Fairy

icely Mary Barker celebrated the longevity of the poppy with her Poppy Fairy poem, mentioning that the flower stands proud in fields alongside wheat when it is green but also after the crop is harvested. In addition, Barker created an illustration and a poem for the Shirley Poppy Fairy, clothed in pink like the flower. The Shirley Poppy was created by a vicar in Shirley, south London, which neighbours Barker's home area of Croydon.

Once upon a time…

The Poppy Fairy has gone on to have various incarnations after Cicely Mary Barker's original creation. She also included a Horned Poppy Fairy in her *Flower Fairies of the Wayside* book.

Origins:

The first appearance of the Poppy Fairy was in Cicely Mary Barker's early book, *Flower Fairies of the Summer*, dating from the 1920s.

In popular culture:

There are many modern variations on the Poppy Fairy in books, including a Rainbow Magic Petal Fairies one from Daisy Meadows. You can also buy felt Poppy Fairies, metal Poppy Fairies and Poppy Fairies to assemble yourself.

The Primrose Fairy

 here has long been an association between primroses and fairies. It is said that if you touch a 'fairy' rock with the right number of primroses in a posy, it will open to fairyland. But the wrong number will open the door of doom. Cicely Mary Barker illustrated a primrose fairy. Influenced by the Pre-Raphaelites, her style of fairies has been much imitated.

Once upon a time…
According to Scottish legend, if you want to see a fairy, you must eat a primrose.

Origins:
There is a plant called a fairy primrose. Also known as the baby primrose, *Primula malacoides* is native to Asia and usually has purple flowers. A European version is called *Primula minimosa*.

In popular culture:
In recent years, real-life humans have adopted the 'Primrose Fairy' moniker: *Primrose the Fairy* tours the USA and has more than 100,000 followers on Facebook, while *The Primrose Fairy* has a YouTube crafting channel and more than 700 subscribers.

An evening primrose fairy in the style of Cicely Mary Barker,
also, like hers, in the yellow variety of the flower

"To walk in nature is to witness a thousand miracles"

— *Mary Davis*

"I believe in everything until it's disproved. So I believe in fairies, the myths, dragons. It all exists, even if it's in your mind. Who's to say that dreams and nightmares aren't as real as the here and now?"

— *John Lennon*

Illustration by H J Ford from The Violet Fairy Book
by Andrew Lang (1901)

The Violet Fairy

 iolet is a popular colour for fairies, possibly because in 1901 Scottish poet and anthropologist Andrew Lang published a book of folk tales called *The Violet Fairy Book*, with a purple cover. Cicely Mary Barker also produced a Dog-Violet Fairy, the 'dog' part of this violet's name referring to its lack of scent, 'dog' being used to denote something that is inferior to another variety.

Once upon a time…
In the Victorian language of flowers, if you were given a purple violet, this indicated that the sender's thoughts were occupied by love.

Origins:
To ensure that her illustrations were botanically accurate, Cicely Mary Barker arranged for Kew Gardens to bring her specimens to copy, and one of her models would pose holding it.

In popular culture:
British musician Laurel named the Dog-Violet Fairy as one of her favourite Flower Fairies. She has been obsessed with them since she was young and named her 2018 debut album DOGVIOLET.

The Wild Cherry Blossom Fairy

herry blossom is a much-appreciated spring phenomenon all over the world, particularly in Japan, where the cherry blossom is the national flower and is central to the custom of *hanami* (flower viewing). Cicely Mary Barker produced a Wild Cherry Blossom Fairy in her 1940 book *Flower Fairies of the Trees* and the fairy was contained in a postcard book that sold during the Second World War.

Once upon a time…
In Highland folklore, to chance upon a wild cherry was considered auspicious and fateful. In Japan, the cherry tree represents good fortune, new beginnings and revival.

Origins:
Cicely Mary Barker was heavily influenced by the Pre-Raphaelite Brotherhood and shared their desire to represent life 'true to nature'. As part of this, she made the costumes that her child models wore when they posed for her.

In popular culture:
Coincidentally, there is a Cherry Blossom variety of Fairy washing-up liquid.

*Cherry blossom — sakura — is the national flower of Japan
and is central to the custom of flower viewing — hanami.*

"If you've never been thrilled to the very
edges of your soul by a flower in spring
bloom, maybe your soul has never been
in bloom."

— *Audra Foveo*

The Fern Fairy

irth of the Fern Fairy is an illustration from a popular children's book from circa 1880 called *A Keepsake for the Young – A Book of Amusement* under the name Aunt Friendly. The book was published by Frederick Warne, who is known for originally turning down Beatrix Potter. But when his sons took over his firm as he aged, they published her works. The fern fairy illustration was so liked that it was reproduced as a jigsaw.

Once upon a time…
Ferns are widely associated with magic because of the conundrum of how they reproduce with no flowers and no seed.

Origins:
A Keepsake for the Young – A Book of Amusement also portrayed Biblical stories, as there is an illustration in it of the blessing of Jacob.

In popular culture:
One of Frederick Warne's sons, Norman, was portrayed by Ewan McGregor in the 2006 film *Miss Potter*, about the publishing of Beatrix Potter's works. Beatrix Potter was played by Renee Zellweger.

The Lily Fairy *by Luis Ricardo Falero,*
1888. Like ferns, lilies enjoy moisture
and shade

"The world can give you these glimpses
as well as fairy tales can — the smell
of rain, the dazzle of the sun on white
clapboard with the shadows of ferns and
wash on the line."

— *Frederick Buechner*

"*Beauty is a fairy; sometimes she hides herself in a flower-cup, or under a leaf, or creeps into the old ivy, and plays hide-and-seek with the sunbeams, or haunts some ruined spot, or laughs out of a bright young face.*"

— George Augustus Henry Sala

19th century engraving of the Ivy Fairy

The Ivy Fairy

As an evergreen, ivy has long been imbued with spiritual significance, and it was brought into homes to drive out evil spirits. As it clings, and remains green, it is seen as a symbol of lasting love and friendship. Cicely Mary Barker produced a ground-ivy fairy, making the distinction between it and common ivy, the former being more traditionally attractive and boasting flowers.

Once upon a time…
Barker did not see any conflict between illustrating fairies and being a devout Christian. She was described as 'one of the pillars' of St Andrew's Church, Croydon, and designed cards for Christian causes and panels for churches.

Origins:
One of the models for Cicely Mary Barker's fairies was the appropriately named Gladys Tidy, the young girl who visited the Barker house every Saturday to do the household work.

In popular culture:
Videos of Cicely Mary Barker's books being flicked through now abound on YouTube.

"*People who have had fairy encounters often speak of the opalescent, light-filled quality of fairies. Their luminescent aspect gives rise to the name 'the Shining Ones'.*"

— *Sirona Knight*

Jasmine fairy is also a type of Chinese tea, so named because the jasmine flowers dance in the water like fairies

The Jasmine Fairy

he jasmine flower has many uses around the world – such as in tea, rice or in garlands – and is a national symbol of a number of countries. Cicely Mary Barker created a jasmine fairy, which has had a rebirth in the 21st century with the book *Jasmine's Starry Night* by Kay Woodward, but based on Barker's original. Barker also created a winter jasmine fairy.

Once upon a time…

Jasmine has long been associated with the night – and is even called 'Queen of the Night' – as that is when the flower's scent is most potent, referenced in Barker's poem for Jasmine.

Origins:

Barker loved to be inspired by plants in the garden of the home where she grew up, but also in Swanage, in Dorset, and Whitby, in Yorkshire, where she was taken on holiday.

In popular culture:

Many Flower Fairies images are free to download on the internet as PNG files.

Moon Princess

oon Princess is a fairy tale written by Edith Ogden Harrison and published in 1905 that tells the story of a young princess who discovers her celestial origins. A writer of children's books and fairy tales, she was the wife of Carter Harrison Jr, who was mayor of Chicago for five terms. Originally from New Orleans, she was a friend of L. Frank Baum, who wrote the original *Wonderful Wizard of Oz book* and its 13 successors.

Once upon a time...
Fairies are often associated with the moon, as it is seen as a link between the mortal and magical worlds.

Origins:
Previous to *Moon Princess*, in 1903 Edith Ogden Harrison's interest in fairies and the heavens had resulted in a collection of stories under the title *The Star Fairies and Other Fairy Tales*.

In popular culture:
Moon fairies have made their way into the world of Barbie and are one of seven types of fairies in found in Barbie's *Fairytopia* universe of animated films.

Fairies are said to be fond of coming out at night and dancing by the light of the moon

"Then I remembered that night is the fairies' day, and the moon their sun, and I thought — Everything sleeps and dreams now: when the night comes, it will be different."

— George MacDonald

The Lilac Fairy

he Lilac Fairy is notable in Tchaikovsky's ballet of the *Sleeping Beauty* story. The 19th century Russian composer worked on the plot for his version with Ivan Vsevolozhsky, the pair taking Charles Perrault's 17th century telling of the fairy tale as their base material. In the ballet, the Lilac Fairy prevents the story's evil fairy from condemning main character Aurora to death, instead sending her into a sleep from which a prince can awaken her.

Once upon a time…
In Perrault's story, the fairy was one of seven to be invited to Aurora's Christening, to be her godmothers.

Origins:
The earliest versions of the Sleeping Beauty tale are in the 14th century works *Perceforest*, in French, and *Frayre de Joy e Sor de Plaser*, in Catalan.

In popular culture:
A dark lilac variety of a primrose has been named after the Lilac Fairy, *Primula x pubescens* 'Lilac Fairy'.

A lilac fairy with much on her mind and partly encircled by the moon.

"For three hours I lived in a magic dream, intoxicated by fairies and princesses, by splendid palaces streaming with gold, by the enchantment of fairy-tale."

— *Pyotr Illyich Tchaikovsky, on his* Sleeping Beauty *ballet*

"*If you see a fairy in a field of grass very lightly step around, tiptoe as you pass; last night fairies frolicked there, and they're sleeping somewhere near.*"

—*William Shakespeare*

A John Simmons painting from the 1860s of Titania sleeping in the moonlight, protected by her fairies

Titania

n Shakespeare's *A Midsummer Night's Dream*, Titania is the Queen of the Fairies and the wife of Oberon, the Fairy King. Together they guarantee the fertility of the human and natural worlds, but they spend much of the play in disagreement. In the play, a spell is cast on Titania by Oberon's servant Puck, and she becomes enamoured with Nick Bottom, a 'rude mechanical' whose head has been turned into that of a donkey.

Once upon a time…
Because using overtly pagan names drew accusations of witchcraft in Shakespeare's time, he chose classical names for Oberon and Titania.

Origins:
Shakespeare took Titania's name from Ovid's *Metamorphoses* – it is used to refer to the daughters of Titans in the work.

In popular culture:
Dr Andrew Doyle used Titania as the first name for his spoof social media account that lampooned those obsessed with identity politics. He said that the character he invented was a 'militant vegan who thinks she is a better poet than William Shakespeare'.

"Fairies, come take me out of this dull world, for I would ride with you upon the wind, run on the top of the dishevelled tide, and dance upon the mountains like a flame."

— *W.B. Yeats*

Tinker Bell on the cover of J.M. Barrie's Peter Pan and Wendy,
with the two main characters

Tinker Bell

inker Bell is a character from J.M. Barrie's 1904 play *Peter Pan* and its novelization five years later, *Peter and Wendy*. Such was the success of the animated 1953 Disney film *Peter Pan* – and Tinker Bell's role in it – that her image has become an unofficial mascot of The Walt Disney Company. She is also the centrepiece of the Disney Fairies media franchise, which includes a *Tinker Bell* film series.

Once upon a time...
In the original, Tinker Bell's wayward emotions are explained by fairies being so small they can hold only one feeling at a time.

Origins:
J.M. Barrie's creation is a fairy who mends pots and kettles, so she is literally a fairy who is a tinker. And her speech consists of the sounds of a tinkling bell, only understandable to those who know fairy language.

In popular culture:
The first Peter Pan film was released in 1924 and Tinker Bell was played by the appropriately named Virgina Brown Faire.

Princess Ozma

rincess Ozma is a character from L. Frank Baum's *Land of Oz* and she appears in every book in the *Oz* series apart from the first, 1900's *Wonderful Wizard of Oz*. There are 14 books in the *Oz* series but it was not until the ninth, *The Scarecrow of Oz*, that Baum revealed that Princess Ozma was a fairy and descended from a 'long line of fairy queens'.

Once upon a time…
Princess Ozma is the rightful ruler of Oz, but she is given to the witch Mombi and transformed into a boy.

Origins:
Baum originally described her as having hair that was 'ruddy gold' in colour, and she was illustrated as such, but later illustrations made her hair darker.

In popular culture:
The look of Padme Amidala, who was played by Natalie Portman in episodes 1–3 of the *Star Wars* films, was based on Princess Ozma.

Princess Ozma illustrated by John Rea Neill
for L. Frank Baum's Oz books

"It is not children only that one feeds
with fairy tales."

— *Gotthold Ephram Lessing*

"We cannot, of course, disprove God, just as we can't disprove Thor, fairies, leprechauns and the Flying Spaghetti Monster."

— Richard Dawkins

The actress Priscilla Horton as Ariel in Shakespeare's The Tempest *in 1837*

Ariel

riel is a spirit in Shakespeare's play *The Tempest* who serves the magician Prospero, and whose powers create the storm of the title. For the duration of the play, Ariel is Prospero's spy, watching over the activities of the people he has shipwrecked in the storm. Ariel was written as a male part, but from the 17th to the 20th centuries, women chiefly were cast in the role.

Once upon a time...
During the Renaissance, a common view of sprites such as Ariel was that they were agents of the Devil or agents of God, but a more scientific view was that they were neutral beings who could be brought under control by the wise.

Origins:
Shakespeare's stage directions for *The Tempest* are particularly precise, revealing how Ariel was conjured on stage and how his magic was conveyed.

In popular culture:
The 1956 film *Forbidden Planet* – which spawned a stage musical, *Return to the Forbidden Planet* – was based on *The Tempest* and had a robot called Robby in the role of Ariel.

The Cottingley Fairies

he 'Cottingley Fairies' appear in a series of five photographs taken in 1917 by Elsie Wright and Frances Griffiths, two young cousins who lived in Cottingley, in Yorkshire, England. Sir Arthur Conan Doyle used them to illustrate an article on fairies for *The Strand Magazine* and the pictures received much attention over the years, with some saying they were proof fairies existed. In the 1980s, Elsie and Frances admitted the fairies were cut-outs from a children's book, but Frances maintained one photograph was genuine.

Once upon a time...
Sir Arthur Conan Doyle said the photographs were evidence of psychic phenomena, and in 1966, Elsie hinted that she had photographed her thoughts.

Origins:
The girls originally took the photographs to justify their claim to their family that the only reason they were playing in the muddy beck at the bottom of the garden was to see the fairies.

In popular culture:
Two 1997 films, *Fairy Tale: A True Story* and *Photographing Fairies*, were inspired by the Cottingley Fairies story.

Frances Griffiths in 1920 with one of the cut-out fairies
she made with cousin Elsie Wright

"There are fairies at the bottom
of our garden."

— *Rose Fyleman*

The Blue Fairy

he Blue Fairy is a character in Carlo Collodi's 1883 children's novel *The Adventures of Pinocchio*. She adopts Pinocchio – a puppet who has been brought to life – first as her brother and then as her son. Written in the novel as a fairy with turquoise hair, she was called the Blue Fairy in the 1940 Disney animated film of the story.

Once upon a time…
The Blue Fairy is instrumental in Pinocchio finally becoming a real boy.

Origins:
In the original Italian, the Blue Fairy's name is La Fata dai Capelli Turchini.

In popular culture:
The Blue Fairy has been played on screen – in TV and film – by Gina Lollabrigida, Julia Louis-Dreyfus, Cynthia Erivo, Rickie Lee Jones and Glenn Close. Other Blue Fairy types of character have been played by Meryl Streep, Genevieve Bujold and Tilda Swinton.

An illustration from the Pinocchio story showing the Blue
Fairy commanding birds to peck Pinocchio's nose shorter.

"I think that fairy tales, old ones
and new ones, can help to educate the
mind. Fairy tales are the place
of all hypotheses."

— Gianni Riodari

"*Obsessed by a fairy tale, we spend our lives searching for a magic door and a lost kingdom of peace.*"

— *Eugene O'Neill*

Queen Mab from Peter Pan in Kensington Gardens, *illustration by Arthur Rackham*

Queen Mab

ueen Mab is referred to in Shakespeare's *Romeo and Juliet* as 'the faeries' midwife' but later depictions have cast her as the Queen of the Fairies. She is mentioned in the play by Mercutio, who says she has a whip made from 'cricket's bone' and a chariot that is an 'empty hazelnut', and that she is no bigger than an 'agate-stone' on the 'fore-finger of an alderman'.

Once upon a time...

Debate abounds as to whether Queen Mab is purely of Shakespeare's invention or whether she is based on a character from folklore.

Origins:

A possible precursor to Mab is Medb, a legendary queen from 12th century Irish poetry. Or she could stem from the common name Mabel and the fact that, in Shakespeare's time, names of fairies tended to be generic and monosyllabic.

In popular culture:

Queen Mab often appears in TV shows, novels and music, but she also is the subject of 19th century poet Percy Bysshe Shelley's first large work, *Queen Mab*.

The Bluebell Fairy

luebells can cover woodland floors in spring and the magical sights have gone hand-in-hand with stories of fairies there. Faries are said to hang their spells on the flowers, and if you pick or step on a bluebell you will break its spell and the spirits will become upset. It is also believed that children can be abducted by fairies if they walk into a bluebell wood. Cicely Mary Barker had a Bluebell Fairy in her collection.

Once upon a time...
Bluebell woods have long been associated with fairies and it is said that if you hear a bluebell ring, you will be visited by a bad fairy, and will die not long after.

Origins:
There is a belief that if you wander into a ring of bluebells, you will fall under fairy enchantment.

In popular culture:
There are numerous children's books featuring fairies called Bluebell, including a Disney one and a 'Fashion Fairy Princess' called Bluebell.

*An illustration of a bluebell fairy – bluebells and fairies
are intertwined in folklore*

*"The bluebell is the sweetest flower
that waves in summer air; its blossoms
have the mightiest power to soothe
my spirit's care."*

— Emily Bronte

Fairies from Folklore

The fairies that surround us all stem from the folklore of wherever
we are, but some countries are particularly spoilt for choice
when it comes to the range of spirits on offer. Ireland and Wales
have very strong fairy traditions, as does the rest of Britain, and
much of Europe. And emigration from these countries has taken
European beliefs far and wide, where they mingle with fairy lore that
developed by itself across the other continents.

*Two fairies, one of which is Puck, on the right,
in a 1908 Arthur Rackham illustration.*

Fairy Godmother

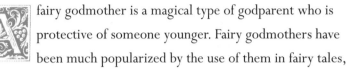 fairy godmother is a magical type of godparent who is protective of someone younger. Fairy godmothers have been much popularized by the use of them in fairy tales, such as the ones written by the 17th century French author Charles Perrault. With so many such stories being made into films in the 20th and 21st centuries, the modern image of a fairy godmother is most likely one from animated Disney movies such as *Cinderella* or *Sleeping Beauty*.

Once upon a time...
Fairy godmothers are named after the role godparents play in Christian traditions, but many non-Christian societies have had similar roles for thousands of years.

Origins:
The fairy godmother has her roots in the Greek Fates, who ensured humans live their lives as decreed by the universe. This is seen particularly in *Sleeping Beauty*, in which the fairies determine how Aurora's life should be lived.

In popular culture:
Disney's *Sleeping Beauty* has three fairy godmothers, based on Perrault's version of the tale.

Image from the 1910 book The Sleeping Beauty
and other Fairy Tales from the Old French

"I think, at a child's birth, if a mother
could ask a fairy godmother to endow
it with the most useful gift, that gift
should be curiosity."

— Eleanor Roosevelt

"For there is nothing lost, that may be found, if sought."

— *Edmund Spenser, from his poem* The Faerie Queen

Painting of Prince Arthur and the Fairy Queen
by Johann Heinrich Füssli

Fairy Queen

I n folklore, the Fairy Queen is the ruler of the fairies, sometimes with a king, sometimes without. Many names are given to her, Titania one, from Shakespeare's *A Midsummer Night's Dream*, and Mab another, from his *Romeo and Juliet*. Fairy queens exist in tales around the world, but they are particularly prevalent in Irish and British tales, and also in Greek folklore.

Once upon a time…
Some of the most well-known fairies have been fairy queens, such as the Arthurian Morgan le Fay.

Origins:
The Roman goddess Diana is often seen as a fairy queen. She was the goddess of hunting, fertility, nature, the night and the moon.

In popular culture:
Frank Baum included a fairy queen in his *Oz* books, Queen Lurline, who helped to create the Land of Oz and is the mother of fairy Princess Ozma. Lurline's name is based on the Lorelei, the treacherous Rhine nymphs.

Puck

n English folklore, Puck is a fairy known for playing pranks, who is also known as Robin Goodfellow. Puck has been popularised by Shakespeare's play *A Midsummer Night's Dream*, in which he is also referred to as Robin Goodfellow. In addition, Puck may also be called a Hobgoblin. Although a good fairy, in the 19th century some people saw him more as a devil, because of his mischievous nature.

Once upon a time…

Debate continues as to whether Puck stemmed from Celtic folklore and spread from there, or whether he was evident in Norse tales first.

Origins:

Many European languages have a word for their own version of Puck. In Irish and Old English, he is Puca, in Old Norse and Icelandic Puki, in Old Swedish Puke, in Welsh Pwca and in Cornish Bucca.

In popular culture:

Robin Goodfellow is mentioned in an 1856 speech by Karl Marx, who championed Puck's subversive nature.

Arthur Rackham 1908 illustration of Puck from the text of
A Midsummer Night's Dream

"Now a house, now an ass, now a bull,
now a goat, now an eagle"

—W.B Yeats, on the many forms of 'Puca'

Nuala

uala is a shortened form of Fionnuala, who is the wife of Ireland's fairy king, Finvarra. Nuala/Fionnuala is also the daughter of Lir, an Irish sea god, and her name means 'born of the sea'. In the legend the *Children of Lir*, she was changed into a swan and cursed by her stepmother to wander the rivers and lakes of Ireland for 900 years with her brothers.

Once upon a time…

Nuala's father Lir is one of the Tuatha De Danann, a race of mythological Irish beings who live in the 'otherworld' but access our world via burial mounds.

Origins:

In the *Children of Lir*, Nuala and her brothers were condemned to spend 900 years as swans but retained the power of speech and were able to sing of their fate.

In popular culture:

On Sinead O'Connor's 1994 album *Universal Mother*, the song 'A Perfect Indian' contains a reference to 'Lir's children'.

*An 1780 engraving by Francesco Bartolozzi of Una,
one of the many fairies to have 'queen' status*

*"Miracles are made of wings you forgot
were on your back."*

— *Fiadhnait Moser*

"Like many evil and cruel women, Morgan Le Fay knew men's weaknesses and discounted their strengths. And she knew also that most improbable actions may be successful so long as they are taken boldly and without hesitation."

— *John Steinbeck*

An 1864 painting of Morgan-le-Fay by British Pre-Raphaelite Frederick Sandys

Morgan-le-Fay

organ Le Fay is an enchantress from the legend of King Arthur who is seen as good by some and evil by others. The first documented account of her was in Geoffrey of Monmouth's 12th century *Vita Merlini*, in which she was unrelated to King Arthur, but later texts pinned her as King Arthur's elder sister. In Sir Thomas Malory's *Le Morte d'Arthur*, she is portrayed as having many lovers but suffering unrequited love for Lancelot, and hating Arthur's wife Guinevere.

Once upon a time…
In *Vita Merlini*, and in tales told by Chretien de Troyes, Morgan Le Fay's chief role is as a healer.

Origins:
The 'Le Fay' part of Morgan's name comes from the French 'Le Fee', meaning "The Fairy".

In popular culture:
Morgan Le Fay is one of the most popular fairy characters in modern culture, and usually portrayed as evil. She spans film, television, comics, video games and books.

"The fey wonders of the world only exist while there are those with the sight to see them."

— *Charles de Lint*

A print from circa 1900 showing Oberon and Titania from A Midsummer Night's Dream

Oberon

n medieval England, Oberon was known as the king of the fairies and Shakespeare used his name for his fairy king in *A Midsummer Night's Dream*. He is small in height but very handsome and carries a magical cup, which can produce food as well as wine. His beauty was given as compensation for his small stature. The name Oberon is a variant of Auberon.

Once upon a time…
The first record of Oberon is in a 13th century French song, in which he is described as the son of Morgan Le Fay and Julius Caesar.

Origins:
In the folklore of Oberon, the fairy king says that he was cursed not to grow beyond the age of three by a female fairy, one of the earliest examples of a wicked fairy godmother.

In popular culture:
The two largest moons of Uranus are named Oberon and Titania, who is Oberon's wife in *A Midsummer Night's Dream*.

Knockers

nocker is a subterranean creature from the folklore of the English counties of Cornwall and Devon. In Cornwall he is described as having an oversized head for his short stature, and long arms and wrinkled skin. He wears miners' clothes and steals their food and tools, and creates other mischief. In the US, Knockers are known as Tommyknockers, the tradition having been brought over the Atlantic by British immigrant miners.

Once upon a time...
Pre-industrial miners in Devon and Cornwall believed that Knockers led them towards veins of tin, and that Knockers would also bang on tunnel walls to warn the miners of impending collapse.

Origins:
Similar to Knockers are Brownies, the Welsh Coblynau, Irish Leprechauns and Klokers, from the county of Kent.

In popular culture:
Author Stephen King named his 1987 book *The Tommyknockers* after the creatures.

Knockers are similar to goblins, and a Welsh type, coblynau, has a goblin-like name

"In all likelihood fairies of larger stature were ancient gods in a state of decay, while their diminutive congeners were the swarming spirits of primitive imagination."

— Lewis Spence

"I've always believed in good witches
— not bad witches — and fairies and
angels."

— Stevie Nicks

An 1880 Gustave Moreau painting of Nyx, the 'Night Goddess',
as opposed to Nix, the water sprite

Nix

Nix is a shapeshifting water spirit from Germanic folklore, with 'Nix' being the male version and 'Nixe' being a river mermaid. Nix are also common in Scandinavian mythology, where they are called Nock in Norwegian and Nack in Swedish. Nix are not to be confused with Nyx, who is the personification of night in Greek mythology and who has been portrayed in a Tinker Bell film and a *Final Fantasy* computer game.

Once upon a time…
In the Faroe Islands, a version of the Nix – the Nykur – refers specifically to a supernatural horse who lives in water.

Origins:
Melusine in France, Xana in Spain and Rusalka in Slavic countries are very similar spirits to the Nix, showing how the phenomenon exists across Europe from east to west.

In popular culture:
In the 2019 *Frozen II*, Queen Elsa tames a Nokk in the form of a horse.

Will-o'-the-Wisp

ill-o'-the-Wisp is a ghostly fairy seen by travellers at night, often hovering over marshes, bogs and swamps. Other names for the phenomenon include Jack-o'-Lantern and Friar's Lantern, as the fairy resembles a flickering lamp. People in Europe, the Americas and Asia are familiar with the spirit, as a scientific explanation suggests that the dancing light is created by gases produced by wetlands.

Once upon a time...
The folk legend has, over the generations, come to describe a hope or desire that leads one on but is impossible to reach.

Origins:
A wisp is a bundle of sticks used as a torch, so Will-o'-the-Wisp means the desire of the light.

In popular culture:
The Will-o'-the-Wisp phenomenon made its way on to British television in the form of *Willo the Wisp*, a cartoon series set in a woodland, with actor Kenneth Williams voicing the characters in a 1981 outing and James Dreyfus in a 2005 one.

A circa 1830 depiction of Will-o'-the-Wisp, who populates marshes and swamps

"If happiness always depends on something expected in the future, we are chasing a will-o'-the-wisp that ever eludes our grasp, until the future, and ourselves, vanish into the abyss of death."

— *Alan Wilson Watts*

Joan the Wad

oan the Wad is the queen of the Pixies from the English county of Cornwall. She also has the qualities of a Will-o'-the-Wisp, as there is a rhyme that associates her with 'Jack-the-Lantern' and guiding people home with light. Such is her popularity in Cornwall that there is a Joan the Wad figure outside the Joan the Wad and Piskey shop in Polperro in the county.

Once upon a time...
Pixies are particularly concentrated in high moorland areas of the English counties of Cornwall and Devon, although they also inhabit much of the rest of south-west and southern England.

Origins:
A wad is a colloquial term from eastern Cornwall for a torch or a bundle of straw.

In popular culture:
Joan the Wad lucky charms are carried by some people for good luck and she also appears on door knockers as a protective spirit.

A decorative top for a bottle opener in the shape of Joan the Wad
of Cornish folklore

"She was a pixie, a fairy, full of
imagination and in another world."

— Jean Nathan

"If she were going to die, I'd already be screaming. I'm a female bean sidhe. That's what we do."

— *Rachel Vincent, using the Irish spelling of 'banshee'*

Banshees are female creatures of Irish folklore
whose screaming heralds death

Banshee

 banshee is a female spirit from Irish folklore who heralds the death of a family member by shrieking, screaming or wailing. A banshee's eyes are red from continual weeping. Seventeenth century memoirist Ann, Lady Fanshawe – who is said to have produced the first recipe for ice cream in Europe – said she saw a banshee and that the banshee was dressed in white and had red hair.

Once upon a time...

It is said by some that banshees mourn only the deaths of true Irish people and would not carry out their rites over someone of Norman or Saxon origin.

Origins:

The second syllable of the word 'banshee' stems from the Old Irish 'side', which describes the mounds of earth that cover collective graves.

In popular culture:

American author Edgar Allan Poe's story *Cry of the Banshee*, from the 19th century, was turned into a 1970 horror film starring Vincent Price, from which rock band Siouxsie and the Banshees took their name.

"The most wonderful and the strongest things in the world, you know, are just the things which no one can see."

– *Charles Kingsley*

An Arthur Rackham illustration of the 'flowry-kirtl'd Naiades' for Comus *by John Milton*

Naiad

I n Greek mythology, naiads are water nymphs that preside over fountains, wells, springs, streams, brooks and other bodies of fresh water. They are seen as essential to human life; boys and girls would dedicate locks of hair to a local naiad at a spring in coming-of-age ceremonies. There are types of naiads also in Roman, Turkish, Egyptian, Sicilian and Indian folklore.

Once upon a time…

As with many fairies, naiads can be evil as well as good. In Greek mythology, Hylas, of the ship Argo, was abducted by naiads fascinated by his beauty.

Origins:

Naiad comes from the Greek words 'naein', meaning 'to flow', and 'nama', meaning 'running water'.

In popular culture:

Naiads were a favourite subject of the late 19th and early 20th century English painter John William Waterhouse.

Vila

 vila is a Slavic fairy that has been so much part of Czech culture that it has worked its way into a number of place names – Vilice, Vilin and Vilov. There a vila is a female woodland spirit, but other vilas are water or air nymphs, and they may act with malice towards humans. The word 'vilas' has been loosely anglicised as 'the willies', meaning a sense of nervousness.

Once upon a time…
Vilas are also seen as the spirits of women who died before their wedding night.

Origins:
Vilas are the Slavic equivalent of the Valkyries from Teutonic mythology.

In popular culture:
In the Harry Potter books, 'veelas' put men into a trance with their singing and dancing but, when angered, turn into bird-like creatures and launch fireballs from their hands, and in *Harry Potter and the Goblet of Fire*, veelas are the mascots for the Bulgarian team playing the sport of quidditch.

The Wilis, in the ballet Giselle, *are vilas.*
This is John Brandard's painting of their queen.

"Fairies come in all shapes, colours, sizes
and types, they don't have to be fluffy."

— Dawn French

"The realm of fairy-story is wide and deep and high and filled with many things."

— *J. R. R. Tolkien*

*Landvaettir can take the form of trolls, shown here
in* The Princess and the Trolls *by John Bauer*

Landvaettir

andvaettir are Scandinavian spirits related to specific locations and it is believed that their wellbeing is necessary for the land of the area to be fruitful. People would leave food out for them but the adoption of Christianity in Scandinavia outlawed the practice. Modern pagans have taken to landvaettir – called 'guardian spirits of the country' – and venerated them in recent times.

Once upon a time…
In Iceland, landdisir standing stones are respected as being part of being the landvaettir culture. It is seen as inappropriate to mow grass or let children play near them.

Origins:
'Vaettir' can be translated into English as 'wight' or 'being'.

In popular culture:
The four beings identified as the Icelandic landvaettir are on Iceland's coat of arms, its krona coins and the crest of its national football teams.

Dryads

ryads are tree spirits in Greek mythology and they are said to live in the trees themselves. There are various types of dryad that relate to different trees – laurel, apple, ash and walnut, for instance. Very shy around humans, they are only friendly around the goddess Artemis, it is said. They are also spectacularly long-lived, and Eurydice – the well-known wife of Orpheus – was a dryad.

Once upon a time…
The life force of dryads is derived from the tree in which a dryad lives.

Origins:
'Drys' in Greek signifies oak.

In popular culture:
In 19th century English poet John Keats's *Ode to a Nightingale*, he addresses the nightingale as 'light-winged Dryad of the trees'. A fantasy novel by 20th century writer Thomas Burnett Swann set a story about a dryad – *The Dryad-tree* – in modern Florida.

English Pre-Raphaelite painter
Evelyn De Morgan's The Dryad,
from 1884-1885

"She, Dryad-like, shall wear alternate leaf and acorn-ball in wreath about her hair."

— *Alfred, Lord Tennyson*

Plant Devas

lant devas are nature spirits who can be seen by those whose 'third eye' – or 'mind's eye' or 'inner eye' – has been activated. There are numerous different devas and their roles are said to help the world's ecology function. There are millions of devas also living in the sun, and they inhabit the stars too. It is believed that the ones in the sun – solar angels – sometimes visit Earth and can be seen.

Once upon a time…
Plant devas are referred to by followers of the 19th century religion Theosophism but there are similar nature fairies in Indian mythology, called yakshas.

Origins:
The word 'deva' comes from the Sanskrit for a heavenly being.

In popular culture:
A central part of the Beatles song *Across the Universe* is the refrain in Sanskrit 'Jai guru deva om', and the song was the first track on an ecologically minded 1969 compilation album sold to raise money for the World Wildlife Fund.

Statues of devas abound in Hindu and Buddhist visual culture

"*The devas understand the patterns
of climate change better than we do,
because they are the forces behind the
weather and the winds.*"

— Llewellyn Vaughan-Lee

"Blind folk see the fairies. Oh, better far than we, who miss the shining of their wings because our eyes are filled with things we do not wish to see."

— *Rose Fyleman*

Arthur Rackham's illustration of Billy Blind for the 1919 book Some British Ballads

Billy Blind

illy Blind is a household spirit from English and lowland Scottish folklore who appears as a character in ballads. In the ballads he often gives advice to the characters. In Scotland there is a folk character called Blind Harie, and it is speculated that this is the same one. Illustrator Arthur Rackham portrayed Billy Blind as looking like a goblin and dressed in red.

Once upon a time…
In the ballad *Gil Brenton*, Billy Blind advises the hero that his wife is not the virgin beside him, but a woman hiding nearby who is already pregnant.

Origins:
It is thought that Billy Blind could be a 'folk memory' of the god Odin or Woden from Germanic mythology, but showing the deity's more playful side.

In popular culture:
Nick Mohammed – best known as Ted Lasso's kit-man-turned-adversary Nate in the eponymous TV show – plays a fairy called Billy Blind in the Disney+ TV series *Renegade Nell*, about an 18th century highwaywoman.

Persian Peris

eris are winged spirits renowned for their beauty, and belief in them stems from the area that is now Iran. Although coming from Persia, peris are widely recognized among people who speak Turkic languages – such as Turkish and Uzbek – who are spread all across northern Asia. In Kazakhstan, shamans sometimes consult peris, and among the Uyghurs, shamans use peris to heal women who have miscarried.

Once upon a time…
It is said that peris exist in our realm because they have been denied entry into paradise until they complete a penance.

Origins:
The word 'peri' is derived from the Persian word 'par', meaning wing.

In popular culture:
Gilbert and Sullivan's 1882 operetta *Iolanthe* – about a fairy who has married a mortal – is subtitled *The Peer and the Peri*.

A Mughal-style peri dressed in black,
painted by an unknown Indian artist

"*Life itself is the most wonderful fairy tale.*"

— *Hans Christian Andersen*

"*The earliest truth that we're told is that there's a world alongside this world, with spirits, not mortals, an enchanted universe of fairies, wizards, leprechauns and trolls. They are all around us.*"

—*William Holman Hunt*

Cartoon from an original Punch,
February 1887 by Edward Linley

Leprechaun

 leprechaun is a diminutive supernatural being from Irish folklore whom some see as a fairy. They are usually depicted as bearded men who wear a coat and hat and they often have a pot of gold 'at the end of the rainbow'. Irish poet and writer W.B. Yeats championed the leprechaun and led to them becoming popular with the public in the late 19th century.

Once upon a time…
Leprechauns are often shoemakers, and they love practical jokes.

Origins:
The first mention of the word 'leprechaun' is in the eighth century story *Adventures of Fergus son of Leti*. In the story, Fergus falls asleep on a beach and wakes to find three leprechauns dragging him into the water. He captures his abductors, who grant him three wishes in exchange for release.

In popular culture:
Leprechauns straddle culture, from fronting the Lucky Charms cereal brand to lending their name to financial phenomena – 'leprechaun economics'.

Finvarra

invarra is a fairy king from western Ireland who ensures good harvests and rewards mortals with riches. In one story, he led an army against the giant Finn McCool, the being who was said to be responsible for creating Giant's Causeway as stepping stones to Scotland and precipitating the Isle of Man by throwing a lump of rock into the Irish Sea. Good fortune for Finvarra means good crops for those who believe in him.

Once upon a time…
Finvarra has a beautiful queen called Nuala; however, it is said he often steals human women to be his lovers.

Origins:
On Knockma, a hill in County Galway, there is a cairn that is said to be Finvarra's castle.

In popular culture:
A Dutch band called Finvarra play Celtic music and have covered Led Zeppelin's song *The Battle of Evermore*, which references J.R.R. Tolkien's *The Lord of the Rings*.

An illustration of the Fairy King and Queen from 1910,
by an unknown artist.

*"In truth we do not go Faery, we become
Fairy, and in the beating of a pulse we may
live for a year or for a thousand years."*

— James Stephens

Cliodhna

liodhna is queen of the banshees in Irish mythology. She is responsible for the Blarney Stone being associated with the gift of being able to convince with words. Cormac Laidir MacCarthy, the builder of Blarney Castle, asked for her assistance in a lawsuit and she told him to kiss the first stone he found. He did and won his case and incorporated the stone into the castle. Those who kiss it are said to receive the eloquence he did.

Once upon a time…
She is said to have three highly coloured birds who eat apples from an otherworldly tree and whose song heals sick people. And although she is not human, she has a mortal lover, Ciabhan.

Origins:
It is said a precursor to Cliodhna is the Gaulish goddess Clutonda or Clutondae.

In popular culture:
Cliodhna is a character in the computer game *Smite*, in which she is a goddess and villainess.

Crenaia, the Nymph
of the Dargle *by Frederic
Leighton, 1880*

*"Fairies, cross-culturally, share
a relatively broad common
denominator."*

— *Daniela Simina*

"There is a difference between this world and the world of Faery, but it is not immediately perceptible."

— James Stephens

Fairies from folklore, such as Aibell, also feature in poems, such as Sabrina, here, in John Milton's Comus

Aibell

 ibell is the guardian spirit of the O'Brien clan in Ireland. She has a magic harp, the music of which would lead to the death of whoever heard it. Aibell features prominently in the 18th century comic poem *Cuirt An Mhean Oiche* by Brian Merriman, in which she is described as Queen Aibell of the Fairies and presides over a case based on early Irish law.

Once upon a time…
Aibell is the sister of queen of the banshees Cliodhna, and one story about the pair is that Cliodhna turned Aibell into a white cat.

Origins:
The name 'Aibell' likely comes from the Gaelic 'aoibh', meaning beauty.

In popular culture:
Aibell appears in a number of comics that are spin-offs of the *Ghostbusters* films.

"People who lean on logic and philosophy and rational exposition end by starving the best part of the mind."

— W.B. Yeats

There are many rituals involving fire dedicated to Aine,
who represents summer

Aine

ine in Irish mythology represents summer, wealth and sovereignty, and has command over crops and animals. The FitzGerald clan claim her as one of their own, as she was the wife of Gerald FitzGerald. This enabled the clan, who were of Norman origin, to have greater association with Ireland, and enable some to say that they were 'more Irish than the Irish themselves'.

Once upon a time…
In Ireland the feast of Midsummer Night is held in Aine's honour.

Origins:
She is said to be from County Limerick, where there are various rituals involving fire dedicated to her.

In popular culture:
A harpist and singer named after the fairy, Aine Minogue, has a catalogue of songs about Irish fairies.

Coblynau

ike the knockers of Cornish mythology, coblynau are supernatural beings who work in mines in Wales. They wear miniature miners' outfits and work constantly but never finish their tasks. They are said to be one and a half feet tall, very ugly, but often friendly and helpful. The legend of the coblynau has also been exported to America by people of Welsh origin, just as the Tommyknockers originate from the West Country English taking their lore over the Atlantic when they emigrated.

Once upon a time…
Coblynau would help miners to find rich seams of ore.

Origins:
The word 'coblynau' is related to the English word 'goblin'.

In popular culture:
The US-set TV series *Constantine* features coblynau haunting a mine in western Pennsylvania in its second episode, which demon hunter John Constantine has to investigate. Constantine the character is English but the actor who plays him, Matt Ryan, is, like the coblynau, Welsh.

Similar creatures to coblynau exist in Swedish folklore, depicted here by John Bauer in 1911.

"The land of faery, where nobody gets old and godly and grave, where nobody gets old and crafty and wise, where nobody gets old and bitter of tongue."

— W. B. Yeats

Ellyllon

he ellyllon are one of five varieties of Welsh fairies: the bwbachod, the coblynau, the Gwragedd Annwn and the gwyllion. They live in hidden groves and valleys and are called 'Welsh elves' or 'Welsh pygmies' because of their small size. They wear gloves made from the bells of foxgloves and are fond of eating fungi, even poisonous toadstools and mushrooms, along with 'fairy butter', a fungus found on the roots of rotted trees and in limestone crevices.

Once upon a time...
Ellyllon have magical powers that are used to help or hinder, depending on their temperament.

Origins:
The ruler of the ellyllon is Queen Mab, whom Shakespeare wrote about in his play *Romeo and Juliet*.

In popular culture:
American songwriter and keyboard player Ashley Jurgemeyer – a classically trained former member of the British heavy metal band Cradle of Filth – chose Ellyllon as her stage surname.

"*Perhaps Welsh fairies stole children and confiscated their vowels.*"

— *T. Kingfisher*

*Bwbachod are household spirits that are similar to brownies
and very hard-working.*

Bwbachod

 wbachod are Welsh household spirits that are industrious but mischievous. Good-natured, they expect only a bowl of cream for their work, but they dislike priests and teetotallers, on whom they play pranks. One of the spirits frightened a Baptist preacher away from a home in Cardiganshire by appearing as his double. Bwbachod are similar to brownies and hobgoblins, and other varieties of these household spirits are the fenodyree of the Isle of Man.

Once upon a time...
It is said that if you leave cream on the hearth overnight, it will be churned into butter by bwbachod by the morning.

Origins:
Other names for bwbachod are booakers and cottagers.

In popular culture:
Girl Guides can buy 'Bwbachod' woven emblems to wear, harking back to younger Guides being named Brownies - after the household fairies – because part of their duties would be performing household tasks like the spirits do.

*Arthur Rackham often illustrated the earthy aspects
of fairies' habits and traditions.*

*"In all things of nature there is
something of the marvellous."*

— *Aristotle*

"Look deep into nature, and then you will understand everything better."

— Albert Einstein

Gwyllion are malevolent, old, female fairies,
so believed to be related to witches.

Gwyllion

he gwyllion are fairies that haunt roads in the Welsh mountains and lead travellers astray. But they are afraid of knives, which is common to fairies in Welsh culture. Folklorist Wirt Sikes says that Welsh fairies' aversion to knives could be traced back to the sword Excalibur and the role it plays in the primeval world. Meanwhile, Katherine Briggs suggests fairies' traditional vulnerability to cold iron could be the reason.

Once upon a time...
One of the gwyllion is called the Old Woman of the Mountain and she haunts Llanhyddel Mountain in Monmouthshire. She is the ghost of a woman who had been regarded in life as a witch.

Origins:
Gwyllion are native to southern rather than northern Wales.

In popular culture:
One of the gwyllion is the main antagonist in the 2013 animated film *Barbie: Mariposa and the Fairy Princess*. She is a vengeful old woman with grey hair who attacks the crystal fairies.

Gwragedd Annwn

n Welsh folklore, these fairies live beneath rivers and lakes, and dress in green. They have no fish-like qualities, as other water-fairies do, and also are not ocean-dwelling. They herd cattle and their animals are pure white. Welsh black cattle stem from the one animal that the Gwragedd Annwn had left behind when they took their white ones from a farmer.

Once upon a time…
These fairies have a history spanning Wales – they live at the 'Bearded Lake' Llyn Barfog in the north and Crumlyn Lake in the south.

Origins:
Gwragedd Annwn were created by Saint Patrick – who was born in Wales – when he travelled from Ireland back to his homeland to meet Saint David. He was verbally abused by a crowd for having deserted Wales, whereupon he turned the men into fish and the women into lake fairies.

In popular culture:
Gwragedd Annwn are termed the 'Wives of Hell' in a *Ghosts and Folklore of Wales* podcast.

The Arthurian Lady of the Lake story – illustrated here at Llyn y Fan Fach – is related to the Gwragedd Annwn.

"*The significance of a myth is not easily to be pinned on paper by analytical reasoning.*"

— *J. R. R. Tolkien*

Hobgoblin

I n pre-Christian days, hobgoblins – from English folklore – were considered benevolent, but came to be seen as more mischievous. Shakespeare calls his character Puck in *A Midsummer Night's Dream* a hobgoblin. Small, brown, hairy little men, they are termed 'household spirits' because it is thought they do chores around the home – such as dusting or ironing – when the rest of the inhabitants are asleep, and they are rewarded with food.

Once upon a time...
Types of hobgoblin are Billy Blind (from England and lowland Scotland), Blue Burches (from Somerset) and Robin Roundcap (from East Yorkshire).

Origins:
The first use of the written word 'hobgoblin' can be traced to 1530, but it is thought to have been used in a verbal context long before that.

In popular culture:
Dobby is a type of hobgoblin from Lancashire and Yorkshire and he made his way into the Harry Potter books and films.

An etching of hobgoblins from 1799 by Spanish artist Goya,
part of his Los Caprichos *series.*

"*A foolish consistency is the hobgoblin
of little minds.*"

— *Ralph Waldo Emerson*

"Nothing can be truer than fairy wisdom. It is truer than sunbeams."

— *Douglas Jerrold*

Malevolent, flying creatures populate fairydom, such as John Milton's Rebel Angels as depicted by Gustave Dore.

Sluagh

he Sluagh are the hosts of the unforgiven dead in Irish and Scottish folklore. Flying through the air, they also pick up people and transport them far away. Sluagh are also called the Underfolk and The Wild Hunt. Some say they are feared more than death itself and that they can be described as 'fae gone amuck'. They are said to make a screeching sound as they fly.

Once upon a time...
It is believed that the advent of Christianity provided the Sluagh with their dual personas – first they were thought of as evil supernatural beings; with Christianity, they became carriers of sinners who had not been redeemed.

Origins:
Their name comes from the Irish 'sluag', meaning 'host', 'assembly', 'crowd' or 'army'.

In popular culture:
In the virtual-reality ride *Battle for Eire* at the Bush Gardens Williamsburg theme park in the US state of Virginia, the Sluagh are the minions of the villain Balor.

"I've always believed in experiencing everything in life. When you walk out with blinders on, you cut yourself off from the angels and the fairies."

— *Alyssa Milano*

The evil seductress that is the baobhan sith is said to wear a long green dress.

Baobhan sith

he boabhan sith is a fairy from the Scottish Highlands who appears as a beautiful woman to seduce her victim before attacking and killing them. According to a Scottish folklorist, she wears a long green dress that covers deer hooves. She also takes the form of a hooded crow or raven. Those said to have been attacked by the baobhan sith are often men going hunting at night.

Once upon a time…

In one baobhan sith story, a hunter is protected by the iron in his horse's hooves, fairies being vulnerable to iron.

Origins:

In baobhan sith stories, she appears immediately after hunters express their desire for female companionship. This is connected to the traditional Scottish belief that if you make a wish at night without invoking God's protection, it would be granted in some terrible manner.

In popular culture:

The 2013 film *Under the Skin* is loosely based on the baobhan sith myth. Scarlett Johansson plays an otherworldly woman who preys on men in Scotland.

Chaneques

haneques are legendary creatures from Mexican folklore, and they are regarded as guardians of nature. Varieties of chaneque exist throughout Latin America and there are similar spirits in the pre-colonial cultures of the Americas. Chaneques are often referred to as 'duende' and the Yucatec Mayan people call chaneques 'Aluxob'. Villagers used to give chaneques offerings in exchange for protection of their crops.

Once upon a time...
In some legends, chaneques are portrayed as children with the faces of the elderly, who lead people astray for several days. Victims experience loss of memory for the period they have been away, explained by them having been taken to the Underworld for that time.

Origins:
The entrance to the Underworld is said to be within a dried kapok tree.

In popular culture:
In 2023, *The Legend of the Chaneques* was made, a Mexican horror-adventure animated film about the creatures.

A small, smiling figure from Mexico dating from the 7th–8th century in the pre-colonial era.

"Up the airy mountain, down the rushy glen, we daren't go a-hunting, for fear of little men."

—William Allingham

"Fiction is written with reality and reality is written with fiction."

– C. JoyBell C.

A 'netsuke' – small Japanese sculpture – of a kappa from the mid 19th century

Kappa

I n Japanese folklore, kappa are supernatural beings that are green and have a turtle-like shell on their back. On their head is a depression filled with water, and if the water is spilled or dries up, the kappa is severely weakened. They have webbed hands and feet, are fond of cucumbers and like to engage in sumo wrestling. They are often accused of assaulting humans in water and removing a mythical organ called a shirikodama from their victim's bottom.

Once upon a time…
'Water sprites' is another translation of 'kappa'.

Origins:
The kappa's name is derived from Japanese words for 'river' (kawa) and 'child' (wappa).

In popular culture:
Sha Wujing, from the 16th century Chinese novel *Journey to the West*, is a kappa. There have been many film, theatre and TV adaptations of *Journey to the West*, including *Monkey*, made for Japanese television, in which Sha Wujing is called Sandy.

Lutin

 lutin is a type of hobgoblin in French fairy tales, with the female creature being called a lutine. They sometimes take the appearance of a horse, ready to ride and saddled, and tangle people's and horses' hair in 'elf-locks'. A version of a lutin is a Nain Rouge, which translates as 'red dwarf', although this has no relation to the type of star of that name, nor the television series which used that moniker.

Once upon a time…

Le Prince Lutin, a 1697 fairy tale written by Marie Catherine d'Aulnoy, describes lutins as being invisible when they want to be and they can be buried in water or earth and still live. They can also move through closed windows and doors.

Origins:

The lutin is similar to the household spirits of England, Germany and Scandinavia, particularly a brownie.

In popular culture:

In Lapland, the assistants of Father Christmas are lutins.

A 1910 Arthur Rackham illustration of a fairy from J.M. Barrie's
Peter Pan in Kensington Gardens

"I myself am a labyrinth, where one easily gets lost"

— Charles Perrault

Koro-pokkuru

oro-pokkuru are a race of small people from the folklore of the Ainu people of northern Japan. The Ainu believe the Koro-pokkuru lived on their land before they did and that they deliver them fish, deer and other game, but always under cover of darkness, as they are not seen. Although the Koro-pokkuru seem to have disappeared from the Ainu landscape, their pits, pottery and stone implements are said to still be scattered around.

Once upon a time…
A story goes that one day a young Ainu man wanted to see a Koro-pokkuru for himself so lay in wait for one as it delivered food. The female Koro-pokkuru was so enraged at being grabbed that her people have not been seen since.

Origins:
A general term for Japanese fairies is Yosei and some of these are so powerful that they can resurrect the dead. Koro-pokkuru sit alongside them in Japanese folklore.

In popular culture:
Koro-pokkuru abound in Japanese popular culture, particularly computer games, comics and animation.

Koro-pokkuru beneath a butterbur *by 19th century Japanese artist Matsuura Takeshiro.*

"At all times, among my friends, both young and old, English or American, I have always found eager listeners to the beautiful legends and fairy tales of Japan, and in telling them I have also found that they were still unknown to the vast majority."

—Yei Theodora Ozaki

"If you take myth and folklore and these things that speak in symbols, they can be interpreted in so many ways that although the actual image is clear enough the interpretation is infinitely blurred."

— Diana Wynne Jones

Yumboes are fond of dancing when the moon is out

Yumboes

umboes are the spirits of the dead in the mythology of the Wolof people, from Senegal, west Africa. Like many supernatural beings in African folklore, they are white in colour. The Yumboes are also said to have silver hair, and are about two feet tall. They dance in the moonlight and feast on large tables, where they are waited on by servants who are invisible but for their hands and their feet.

Once upon a time…
The favourite food of Yumboes is fish, which they catch, and corn, which they steal from humans.

Origins:
Irish writer Thomas Keightley wrote about Yumboes in his 1828 book *The Fairy Mythology*, and remarked on the similarity between Yumboes and European fairies.

In popular culture:
On WizardingWorld.com, a Harry Potter fan website, Yumboes are mentioned as the mascots of the Senegal quidditch team.

"Happily ever after is not a fairy tale. It's a choice."

— Fawn Weaver

A 1504 illustration showing the Weaver Girl looking out in expectation of seeing her lover

Weaver Girl

I n Chinese mythology, Weaver Girl, called Zhinu, is a young woman who has been banished to one side of the 'heavenly river', with the object of her affections, a cowherd, Nulang, being banished to the other, because their love was forbidden. Once a year, a flock of magpies forms a bridge to reunite the lovers. There are versions of this tale in cultures across Asia.

Once upon a time…
It is only on the seventh day of the seventh month each year that the magpies build the bridge between the two lovers.

Origins:
The Arne-Thompson-Uther Index, categorizing folk tales worldwide, classes this tale is type 400: 'The Quest for the Lost Wife'.

In popular culture:
The Weaver Girl story is told in the film *The Karate Kid*, in the US sitcom *The Big Bang Theory*, and is referred to in Carl Sagan's novel *Contact*, about interaction between human and alien life and turned into a film starring Jodie Foster.

Boggart

he 'boggart' is a catch-all term for a spirit, either an indoor or an outdoor one. There are various different spellings for them – they are 'boggarts' in Lancashire but 'boggards' in Yorkshire. They crawl into people's beds at night and put their clammy hands on faces, and they pull on people's ears. Hanging a horseshoe on the door of a house and leaving a pile of salt outside your bedroom are said to keep boggarts away.

Once upon a time…
A boggart is said to always follow a human family, wherever they may flee.

Origins:
The name comes from the Middle English 'bugge', meaning a spirit or monster. And the word is also related to 'bogle', another type of fairy, from which the words 'bogeyman' and 'boogeyman' derive.

In popular culture:
The boggarts in J.K. Rowling's Harry Potter books are shape-shifters that change to resemble the beholder's worst fear.

Unappealing depictions of boggarts reflect how they are linked to bogeymen and boogeymen.

"We must remember that the whole business of seeing fairies is a delicate operation at best. The power to see requires conditions of quiet and peace; and then, fairies are themselves quite as shy as wild creatures and have to be tamed and attracted."

— Dora van Gelder Kunz

"*I have no definite talent or trade,
and how I stay alive is largely
a matter of magic*"

— Charles Bukowski

An Arthur Rackham illustration, The Bogles in the Courtyard,
from the 1918 book English Fairy Tales

Bogle

ogles come from Northumberland and Scotland and are said to exist for the purpose of perplexing mankind rather than seriously harming or serving them. The 'Tatty Bogle' hides himself in a potato field and either attacks unwary humans or causes blight within the patch. This bogle is depicted as a scarecrow, and 'bogle' is an old name for a scarecrow in various parts of England and Scotland.

Once upon a time…

In the Scots poem *The Bogle by the Boor Tree*, a bogle is heard in the wind and the trees to 'fricht wee weans' (frighten small children).

Origins:

The term is derived from the Middle English word 'bugge', from which the term 'bogey' is also derived.

In popular culture:

The bogeyman – or, in America, the boogeyman – is an extension of the bogle and permeates popular culture in books, films and television shows on both sides of the Atlantic.

Lauma

 lauma is a female woodland spirit around the Baltic who cares for orphans. They are part of Lithuanian folklore and appear in the form of goats, bears and dogs, or sometimes a mixture of a human and an animal, with birds' claws and feet. They often have only one eye, like a cyclops, as well as large breasts with stone nipples.

Once upon a time...
Laumas are said to be dangerous to men, and can tickle them to death and then eat their bodies.

Origins:
It is believed that laumas date as far back as the Mesolithic period, just after the last ice age.

In popular culture:
Lauma is a popular first name in Latvia, as well as in Lithuania, and translates from the Latvian as 'fairy'.

A 1980 sculpture of a lauma by Romas Venckus at The Hill of Witches
near Juodkrante, Lithuania.

"Nothing is definite, nothing is finished,
northing is determined."

— Howard Jacobson

"The world calls them its singers and poets and artists and storytellers, but they are just people who have never forgotten the way to fairyland."

— L.M. Montgomery

A painting of a bereginya by Russian artist Andrey Shishkin from 2017

Tokoloshe

I n the Nguni traditional religion of the Zulu, the hairy tokoloshe is a water spirit who can become invisible by swallowing a stone or drinking water. Tokoloshes are mischievous, even evil, and are called upon to cause trouble for others. A tokoloshe has enough power to bring illness upon someone, or even cause their death, it is believed. At its least harmful, the thought of a tokoloshe is used to scare children. They are widely known in southern African culture, appearing in news stories, films and books.

Once upon a time...
A tokoloshe can be summoned by someone approaching a witch doctor for help.

Origins:
In southern African Bantu folklore, people who died at night were thought to have been killed by a tokoloshe. A scientific explanation is that they had suffered from carbon monoxide poisoning from sleeping around a campfire.

In popular culture:
Tokoloshe Man, by South African musician John Kongos, was a 1971 hit single. In the 1990s, British band the Happy Mondays covered it, as they did with his original version of *Step On*.

Mimi

 imis are fairies from Arnhem Land in northern Australia and they are part of the Aboriginal culture there. They have thin, elongated bodies, so much so that they might break in high winds. To avoid this, they spend most of their time living in rock crevices. At night, mimis emerge from the gaps in the rocks with their pets – animals such as crocodiles, kangaroos, butterflies, fish, birds, turtles and pythons.

Once upon a time…
While mimis are mischievous, they are
generally harmless.

Origins:
In Aboriginal folklore, mimis had human form
and created rock paintings before the first
Aboriginal people arrived in northern Australia.
They taught the Aboriginals how to paint, hunt
and cook kangaroo meat.

In popular culture:
A film was made in 2002 called *Mimi*, about
a woman who buys a mimi sculpture
and it comes to life in her home.

Aboriginal rock paintings of mimi-like beings
in Kakadu National Park, Australia

"There are things I want to say that just
simple real-life stories don't let me say."

— *Isobelle Carmody*

"The past is ahead, in front of us."

— Epeli Hau'ofa

A modern-day stamp from New Zealand showing a patupaiarehe,
from the mountains.

Patupaiarehe

atupaiarehe are supernatural beings in Maori mythology who live in the forests and mountains of New Zealand. They are fair-skinned and have fair or red hair and are mostly nocturnal or favour mist and fog as the sunlight can be deadly to them. They like raw food and have an aversion to steam and fire. They have their own buildings but these are invisible to human eyes.

Once upon a time...
Patupaiarehe can actually draw mist around themselves to shroud their skin from sunlight.

Origins:
Another word for patupaiarehe is pakehakeha, which has been suggested to have been derived from pakeha, used to refer to Europeans.

In popular culture:
Patupaiarehe have been the subjects of many television shows and films in New Zealand, as well as songs.

"A day in human life might stretch into years in fairyland."

— *Rosemary Guiley*

*Acalica, who control the weather, appear rarely,
but when they do it is as small, wizened men*

Acalica

calica are winged fairies from Bolivia who live in caves and can control the weather. When they do appear – which is on rare occasions – they do so as wizened, small men. The 'weather fairies' can appear in different colours. They wear leaves and animal fur as clothes and they are left presents by humans of scraps of cloth and ribbon, which they also wear. In exchange for these gifts they can alter the weather.

Once upon a time…
Usually docile creatures, acalica are said to become vengeful or aggressive when someone attempts to upset the balance of nature.

Origins:
Acalica are a variant on weather wixes, who exist in many cultures around the world and are said to be able to control the weather.

In popular culture:
Acalica are dealt with in a YouTube series on extraordinary phenomena called *Exploring Latin X-Files*.

Picture Credits